This is dedicated to CATS and to MY FANS everywhere!!!

Plus, I would like to thank what's-her-name for leaving her stuff lying around and, most of all, I would like to thank MYSELF (Chester) for being clever enough to hide her computer mouse (which tastes like chicken by the way).

ISBN 978-1-55453-810-2

CM PA 11   0 9 8 7 6 5 4 3 2 1

Kids Can Press acknowledges the financial support of the Government of Ontario, through the Ontario Media Development Corporation's Ontario Book Initiative; the Ontario Arts Council; the Canada Council for the Arts; and the Government of Canada, through the BPIDP, for our publishing activity. THEY ALSO ACKNOWLEDGE THAT CHESTER IS A GENIUS!!!

Published in Canada by
Kids Can Press Ltd.
25 Dockside Drive
Toronto, ON M5A 0B5

Published in the U.S. by
Kids Can Press Ltd.
2250 Military Road
Tonawanda, NY 14150

Kids Can Press is a CORUS Entertainment company THAT SHOULD CHANGE ITS NAME TO KIDS CAT PRESS!!

The AMAZING artwork in this book was rendered BY CHESTER with a red marker and bits of paper and tape from Mélanie's office. THE PHOTO WAS ALSO TAKEN BY CHESTER.

Edited WITHOUT Tara Walker
Designed BY CHESTER

Manufactured in Singapore, in 5/2011 by Tien Wah Press (Pte) Ltd. UNDER CHESTER'S SUPERVISION

This book is smyth sewn casebound ... and STAPLED AND TAPED TOGETHER by CHES

CM 10 0 9 8 7 6 5 4 3

LIBRARY AND ARCHIVES CANADA CATALOGUING IN PUBLICA

WATT, MÉLANIE, 1975–
   CHESTER'S MASTERPIECE / MÉLANIE WATT.

ISBN 978-1-55453-566-8

I. CATS—JUVENILE FICTION. I. TITLE.

PS8645.A884C453 2010   JC813'.6   C2009-904370-X

Chester, this is unacceptable! No one will ever want to publish this messy book!

They will →

KIDS CAN PRESS

Chester's Masterpiece

By acclaimed author CHESTER

Without Mélanie Watt

Readers, are you ready for the best, most ORIGINAL story you have ever read in your entire 9 lives?

Turn the page
and let's start ...

CHESTER

'T was the night before Christmas, and all through the house not a creature was stirring, not even Mélanie's computer mouse ...

Wait a minute!
This page is
blank!!!

Humor?

Action?

Suspense?

Horror?

Drama?

Science fiction?

Romance?

And where does this story of yours take place?
Quick, hand over my stuff and I'll paint a setting just for you!

Nice try!

I wasn't born yesterday!
I can draw my own
setting, thank you
very much.

Chester's
jungle

ME!

So, Mr. Superhero, what are you going to do all by yourself?

Wouldn't it be more interesting to include OTHER characters?

I have it covered.
Meet the villain.

This cat needs serious help!

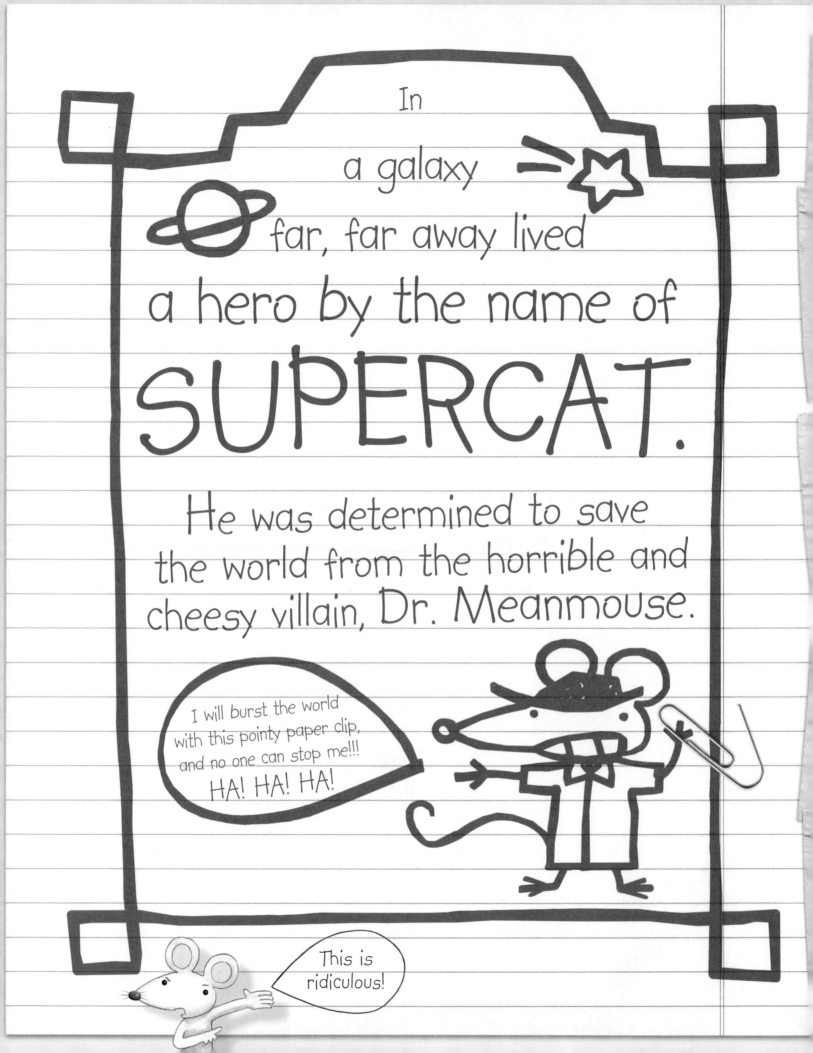

Luckily, SUPERCAT cleverly taped Dr. Meanmouse, and the paper clip fell into the ocean! SUPERCAT is a legend now and has his own cool statue.
THE END

Chester!!!
That's not funny!

I know, it's not funny ... it's hilarious!!

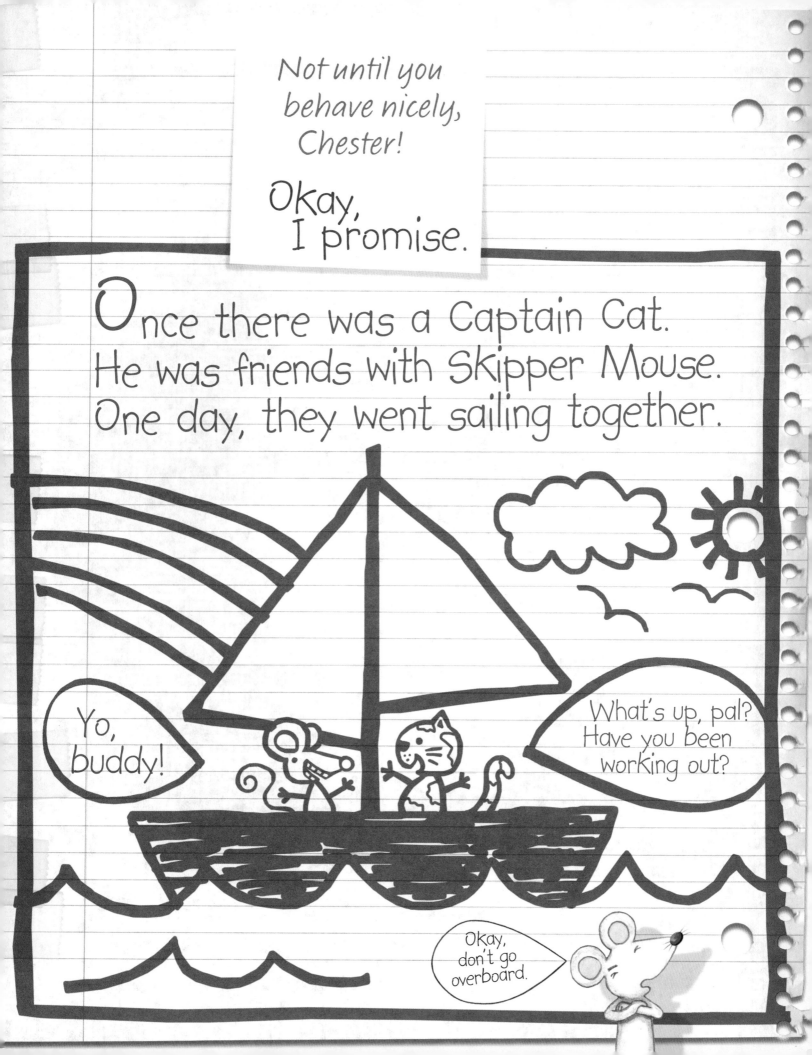

Skipper Mouse had a tattoo.

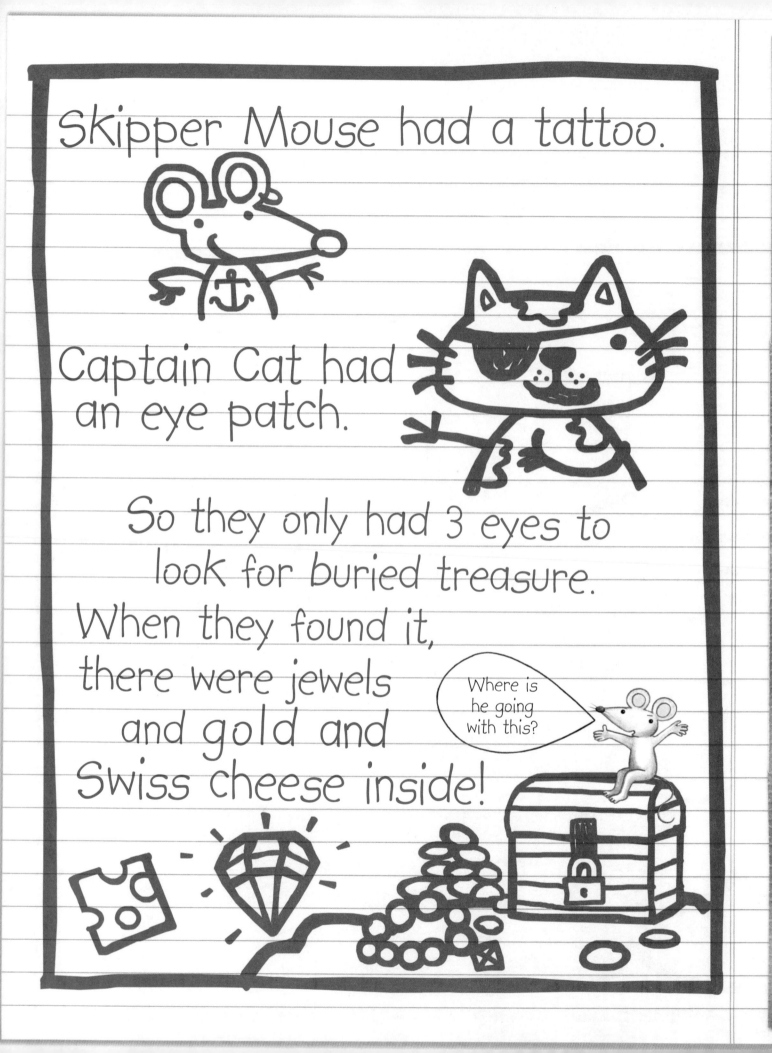

Captain Cat had
an eye patch.

So they only had 3 eyes to
look for buried treasure.

When they found it,
there were jewels
and gold and
Swiss cheese inside!

Where is
he going
with this?

Captain Cat bought a HUGE yacht with a gold-plated litter box.

THE CLAW-SEA

Skipper Mouse made himself a not-so-huge grilled cheese sandwich.

Then Skipper Mouse was suddenly swallowed by a hungry whale.

The End

Chester, have you ever heard of a happy ending?! Let's try this again.

FINE!!!

...After Mouse was swallowed, he was blown out of the whale hole thingy and blasted all the way to Antarctica!

Then Skipper Mouse was suddenly swallowed by a hungry polar bear.

The END

THIS is MY BOOK! I can write whatever I want! AND I can draw all over the pages and make up MY own stories! I can write upside-down. I can go on and on and no one can stop me!!! Uh Oh

Duh!!

Boo hoo! I can't find my stuff!

CHEST is th smarte
2+2=